The New Man
and Other Stories

Adapted by Jeremy Hunter

Series Editor: John McRae

Nelson

Exercises and a glossary can be found at the back of the book.

Thomas Nelson and Sons Ltd
Nelson House Mayfield Road
Walton-on-Thames Surrey
KT12 5PL UK

51 York Place
Edinburgh
EH1 3JD UK

Thomas Nelson (Hong Kong) Ltd
Toppan Building 10/F
22A Westlands Road
Quarry Bay Hong Kong

First published by Thomas Nelson and Sons Ltd 1993

ISBN 0-17-555986-4
NPN 9 8 7 6 5 4 3 2 1

Illustrations by Glyn Rees, Trevor Smith, Stephen May

Adapted from the following stories first published by ALBSU (Adult
Literacy and Basic Skills Unit) in association with Hodder and
Stoughton: *The New Man* by Iris Howden, in *Chillers 4*, copyright 1989;
Cell 13 by Iris Howden, in *Chillers 2*, copyright 1989; and *Carmen
Beach* from *The Collectors* by Marijulia Lloyd, edited by Peter Beynon,
copyright 1990.

Printed in Hong Kong

Contents

PAUL BRYAN
BORN 7 APRIL 1956
DIED 15 JULY 1988

The New Man

The beautiful young woman puts down her flowers. Her husband, tall and dark, stands beside her. He looks at the gravestone.

PAUL BRYAN
Born 7 April 1956
Died 15 July 1988

He knows Paul Bryan's date of birth, and when he died. He knows everything about Paul Bryan very well indeed; better than anybody else. Because he *is* Paul Bryan.

He smiles at his wife. She has tears in her eyes. 'What a good actress!' he thinks. He puts his arm around her shoulders as they walk from the graveyard. 'But I'm a good actor too! Every year, on 15 July, we come here. She puts flowers on the grave, and she cries a little. But not next year!'

He opens the car – a new Jaguar – and they get in.

Then she speaks. 'Can we stop at the Noel Arms for a drink, Mark?' asks the woman.

Mark. Yes, that is his name now. Paul is dead, isn't he? He died in a fire in 1988.

Paul Bryan worked in a factory. In fact, it was *his* factory. 'Bryan and Son'; Paul was the 'Son'. From the time he left school, he worked with his father. The factory was very successful and Paul was very rich.

Paul married Diana in 1986. He was thirty years old. He had everything he wanted. What a lucky man!

Then things went wrong. His father died. The factory started to lose money. 1987 and 1988 were terrible years for Bryan and Son, and for Paul Bryan, the new boss.

Diana changed too. In 1986, she was happy to be the wife of a rich young executive. But two years later she was different. She knew about Paul's problems, but she didn't listen to her husband. Until one night ...

'Start a fire,' said Diana.

'What?' said Paul.

'A fire – at the factory. Burn it to the ground. The insurance will pay us thousands of pounds. We can be rich again, and make a new start. We can leave this town, do something completely different. You know, don't you, Paul, that the factory will never be successful again. But with the insurance money ...'

Diana talked and talked that night. Her head was full of new ideas. And she was a strong woman. Later, in bed, she said to her husband, 'You will do this for me, won't you?' And Paul agreed.

At ten o'clock on Friday evening, 15 July 1988, Paul and Diana went in the Jaguar to the factory. It was only two kilometres away from their house, and nobody saw them.

At one o'clock on Saturday morning, Diana parked her Citroën at a hotel beside the motorway. She used a false name. She was alone.

She went home on Monday morning.

A policewoman told Diana about the fire at the factory on Friday night. Paul's car was outside the factory, and she was very sorry ...

The body was in a toilet on the second floor. It was completely burnt.

When Diana stopped crying, she looked at the policewoman. 'I spoke to him at ten o'clock on Friday,' said Diana. 'He said he was working late.' And she started crying again. For Diana, crying was easy.

After the policewoman left, Diana was very calm again. But she didn't understand why the body was in a second-floor toilet. Because Paul was in his office on the third floor when she locked the door.

'Help! help!' shouted Paul. But he knew that no-one was there. He knew that Diana was not there. He saw her when she locked the door of his office. The office was air-conditioned. The window did not

open. Paul was very frightened. He didn't know what to do.

The fire came into Paul's office. The carpet was burning. Paul was terrified. Then his trousers started to burn ... his shirt ... his jacket. The pain was terrible. Paul ran to the window. He hit the glass with his hand. Nothing happened. He kicked the window with his foot. It still remained firm. The fire now filled the whole office.

Paul hit the window with his head. It broke! His whole body was on fire; and the fire got bigger as the air came in. There was only one thing to do.

Paul jumped from the window. The broken glass ripped his face and body. He fell ten metres to the ground. He was still alive.

He heard the sound of police-cars and fire-engines, and he was frightened again. He had to run. But where?

Paul's mother lived close to the factory. And Paul's younger brother, Jimmy, lived there too. Paul was hurt, very badly, but he had to escape. He felt also that he had to tell Jimmy everything. He needed Jimmy's help.

Diana Bryan was very rich. She got the insurance money from the fire at the factory. She also got the money from Paul's life-insurance policy. At the time of their marriage, Paul insured both their lives for a lot of money.

Diana was rich, but she wasn't happy. She wanted another man: someone to look after her and keep her happy. One year after Paul's death, she sent this advertisement to the *Daily Record*:

> LONELY WIDOW, 27, WISHES TO MEET
> GENTLEMAN, 30 TO 45, FOR FRIENDSHIP.
> BOX 99.
> D. BRYAN

Mark Bowler, aged 33, was drinking a cup of coffee when he read the *Daily Record*. 'What a fool she is!' he thought.

Mark looked into the mirror. Now it was possible to do this. For many months it was not possible. Mark had to avoid mirrors when he was getting better, after the fire. Now he looked completely different. Paul Bryan was dead, but Mark Bowler was alive.

Someone was dead. Who was it – the body in the toilet? A worker who fell asleep? Or a tramp who broke into the factory? It was impossible to know. Diana said that Paul was 'working late'; so everyone thought it was *his* body.

Mark read the advertisement again. Then he wrote a letter to Box 99. He enclosed a photograph of himself.

Mark and Diana met in September 1989. Before Christmas, they were man and wife. Mark felt that he was – again – a lucky man.

The Jaguar leaves the Noel Arms. Diana is driving. She is a terrible driver. The car stops in front of their house. It is a big house. Diana bought the house in 1988 with the insurance money.

Mark is happy. He is happy because Diana is a bad driver. Everyone knows that Diana is a bad driver. So nobody will be surprised when she has a car crash.

When Diana dies, Mark will be a rich man again. The money from her life-insurance policy will come to him. And finally he will get the insurance money from the fire at the factory too. Because Diana is his wife, for the second time.

The same afternoon, Mark phones his brother, Jimmy.

'Hello, Paul,' says Jimmy.

'My name is Mark.'

'OK, Mark.'

Jimmy helped Paul after the fire. Jimmy knew everything. He is a mechanic. He never worked for Bryan and Son.

'Jimmy,' says his brother, 'tomorrow we are going next door for dinner.'

'I understand,' says Jimmy.

'Both the cars will be in the garage.'

'Yes.'

'So – you know – we talked …'

'Yes.'

'Tomorrow evening. OK?'

'OK.'

'I have to take the Jaguar to London the day after. Diana is going to Oxford in the Citroën.'

'OK, I understand,' says Jimmy.

It is evening, on 17 July. A policewoman arrives at the house of Mr and Mrs Mark Bowler. 'I hate this job,' she says to herself.

The door opens.

'Mrs Bowler,' says the policewoman, 'I am very sorry …'

Diana cries. She is a widow for the second time. Mark's Jaguar crashed on the motorway. He is dead.

The policewoman leaves, and Diana makes a telephone call. She is not crying now.

Two hours later, Diana is drinking champagne with Jimmy. 'Well done!' she says.

'I love you,' says Jimmy.

'Turn out the light,' says Diana.

Cell 13

1 March

I hate life in prison. I am a young man. I'm only twenty. I was stupid and now I am paying the price.

There was a man in this cell with me. His name was Jackson. He is free now. He went home this morning. Home, to his family; but I am still here.

It is very quiet, being here alone. There's no-one to talk to. So I am starting this diary. Jackson left his notebook. 'I don't need this now,' he said, when he left. 'You can have it.'

2 March

It is difficult to sleep in this cell, alone. It's too quiet. Jackson always talked to me at night.

Last night I had a bad dream. I thought there was someone standing beside me, wanting me to wake up.

I got a letter from my mother today. Good old Mum! Dad is still ill, so they can't visit me. I hope they can come soon. I will ask them to bring my radio.

3 March

This prison is very old. There are noises in the

night; I hear them when I am trying to sleep. The noises come from the wall: 'knock, knock, knock'.

I think it is Ball making the noise. He is the man in cell 12. I asked him to be quiet. He said to me, 'Don't be stupid!'

Today I got a big bag of old matches. Roberts gave them to me. He works in the canteen. This evening, I started to make a model of a ship. I like to have something to do in the evenings, now I am alone in this cell.

4 March
I can't sleep at all. I'm very tired.

This is my fourth day alone. But there is something strange in this cell. I can hear noises from the other bed. Someone moving in the night. But there's nobody there!

I got a letter from Julie this morning. It makes me sad. She doesn't write often. I don't think she will wait for me. Before I am free, she will marry someone else.

5 March
The ship is quite easy to make. I like making the model in the evenings; the time passes quickly. But I don't like going to bed. I hate the night.

More noises last night. I am sure someone touched my arm. Maybe I am only dreaming. I hope so. Tonight I will try not to sleep. I'll think about my ship for as long as I can.

6 March

Friday. My day in the library. I copied a poem for Julie. She will like it, I think. I want to write her a letter, but I don't know what to say. I can't tell her about the noises at night.

There's an old prisoner working in the library. Smith is his name, but everyone calls him Smithy. He says there is a ghost in my cell! It can't be true.

7 March

Got another letter from my Mum. My father is no better; in fact, he's worse. So they still can't come. Mum says the lawyer can help me. I don't think so. He wants a lot of money, and Mum and Dad don't have a lot of money.

I don't know what to do. I'm so unhappy.

I woke up at five o'clock this morning. I was on the floor! It was very cold and it was still dark. I started to work on my ship. I didn't want to go back to bed.

8 March

I think Smithy is right. Last night there was a voice, a very clear voice. It said my name. 'Jason', it said, into my ear. I was frightened. I started to shout.

O'Dwyer, the prison officer, came to the door of my cell. He told me to be quiet. 'Shut up,' he said. 'Shut up, or we'll stop you watching TV.'

Today is Sunday, so there was chapel. After chapel, I spoke to the priest, Father Donnelly. He is a nice man. He said it is a good idea for me to speak to the doctor. The doctor comes tomorrow.

9 March
The voice came again last night, and a hand touched my arm. I can't stand it!

I asked Bertram, one of the officers, 'Can I see the doctor?'

'OK,' said Bertram, and he opened my door. He is quite kind, not like O'Dwyer.

The doctor thinks I want drugs. He doesn't believe me. No-one believes me. They don't understand that I am alone in cell 13 with a ghost!

10 March
The ship is broken. It's in a thousand pieces. It wasn't me. I didn't do it – it was the ghost!

Bertram was on duty again this morning. I said to him, 'I want to change cells.' But he said that all the other cells were full.

11 March
The ghost was here last night. I saw it, but I still

can't believe my eyes. It was a boy. He was about my age, with fair hair and very white skin. His eyes were pale blue, like ice.

I heard the noise, 'knock, knock, knock'. It came from the corner where the toilet is. He was there! The ghost, standing in the corner and looking at me. He came towards me and touched my arm. My arm is still cold where he touched it.

He didn't say anything.

I don't want to speak to him. I want him to go away.

Another letter from my mother. She didn't mention the lawyer. But she says Dad is worse. 'He's very, very ill,' she says.

12 March

I must change cells. I must speak to the prison governor.

Last night the ghost came again. It was the same boy, with blond hair and blue eyes. He came from the wall, in the corner beside the toilet.

This time he didn't look at me. He stood on the other bed, below the window. He took off his shirt, and put it round the bars of the window. Then he put the shirt round his neck, and jumped off the bed. He hanged himself!

I screamed and shouted. I made a terrible noise. I was terrified!

An officer came. I don't know his name. I tried to explain. But, of course, there was nothing at the window. Only the night sky outside. Then O'Dwyer came too. He said he will see the governor. He wants the governor to give me a punishment. O'Dwyer said that I can't watch TV for a week.

13 March
In the library today, I spoke to Smithy about the ghost. I said the ghost was here. I said it hanged itself. Smithy didn't say anything. He just looked at me. I think he knows something about this ghost, but he won't tell me.

I can see the governor tomorrow. Thank God! I hope he will find another cell for me.

I don't know what will happen tonight.

This is the diary of a young prisoner called Jason Hill. It was on his bed on the morning of Saturday 14 March 1992. The prisoner hanged himself with his shirt on the night of Friday the 13th.

Carmen Beach

Chapter 1

'It is a good idea for students to see things, in real life,' says Professor Ortiz. Ortiz is a professor of biology at the university in Mexico City. 'They learn more quickly when they do things themselves,' he says.

Every year, Professor Ortiz takes a group of students to Carmen Beach. The beach is wide, with golden sand. It is on the Gulf of Mexico, sixty kilometres from Veracruz, the nearest town.

This year the group will spend four days at Carmen Beach. Maria and Anna are students of biology, and they are going on the trip. But Maria is not happy. Anna knows that Maria is not happy. She asks her friend, 'What's the problem, Maria? Don't you like the sea?'

'Oh yes, I like the sea,' replies Maria. 'But don't you know about Domingo?'

'Domingo? Who's he?'

'It's very strange,' says Maria. She looks at Anna with a sad face.

'Come on! Tell me,' says Anna.

'OK. Listen carefully. His name was Antonio Domingo. One weekend, four months ago, he went to the Gulf with an American friend, Clay Connors. They wanted to catch fish. Domingo and Connors stayed on their boat at Carmen Beach. On Sunday they disappeared. Nobody knew where they were. A few days later, Connors returned alone to Veracruz. He didn't remember anything; he didn't know where he was. And nobody saw Domingo again. He disappeared completely. The police looked everywhere, but Domingo never came back.'

'So – a man disappeared. What's the problem? Men disappear for lots of reasons,' says Anna. 'Perhaps the American killed him. Who knows? Why are you worried?'

'I feel bad about this trip,' says Maria.

'Don't be stupid!' says Anna. 'Everything will be fine. And remember, Pablo is coming too.'

Maria smiles. Pablo Ramon is the assistant of Professor Ortiz. He is only twenty-five. Maria likes him very much.

It is the second day of the trip to Carmen Beach. It is five o'clock in the afternoon. The students are staying in tents, close to the sea. Maria is very tired; Anna is not there. She is listening to Professor Ortiz, who is speaking to the students on the beach. Maria wants to sleep, but she can hear the

Professor's voice.

'Now we will go and see some clams. Clams are friendly little animals. They like to live together, in colonies. There is a colony of clams one kilometre up the beach.'

Maria is on the bed. Her eyes are closed.

'Come on, Maria! Get up!' It is a man's voice. Maria opens her eyes, and sees Pablo outside her tent. She is very embarrassed; she starts to go red. Pablo is smiling.

The students are following Professor Ortiz up the beach. Maria goes with Pablo, behind everyone else. She looks into his eyes, and he laughs. He takes her hand. Maria looks at the sand beneath her feet.

As they walk, Pablo stops and points to the sky. 'Professor, look!' he shouts.

Over the Gulf, there is something in the sky. It is far away, but Pablo sees it clearly. It is silver, long and narrow, with red lights on the side.

'Ah yes!' says Professor Ortiz. 'A weather balloon! But we are biologists, not meteorologists. On, on! The clams are waiting.'

Pablo looks at the thing in the sky. There is a noise, and the silver object drops into the sea. Pablo looks very worried.

Maria is worried too. 'That wasn't a weather

balloon,' she says to Pablo.

'No,' says Pablo. 'I'm a scientist, a university assistant. I don't believe in little green men from outer space. But that was a spaceship!'

Maria cannot speak. But there is one thought in her mind – Domingo!

The students arrive at the colony of clams. Professor Ortiz speaks to them for five minutes. Then they begin to walk one kilometre back to their tents. No-one talks about the silver object in the sky, but all of them saw it.

As they walk, the weather changes. The sky is dark, and it is cold. 'What is happening?' says Pablo to himself.

'Funny weather around here,' says Professor Ortiz.

The students return to their tents. Maria wants to sleep, but Anna stays on the beach with the other students. They decide to walk to Carmen village. The village is about three kilometres from the beach. There is a restaurant in the village, and some shops. The students decide to have dinner at the restaurant, and to buy some food for tomorrow.

Anna comes back to her tent. Maria is lying down; she is very tired. Outside, the sky is still dark. It is half-past six.

'We're going to the village,' says Anna. 'Old

Ortiz and his assistant aren't coming. How about you?'

'Are you taking the minibus?' asks Maria.

'No,' says Anna. 'The Prof won't give us the keys. Some problem with insurance. But it's only half-an-hour on foot.'

'I'm too tired,' says Maria. 'I'm sorry. Enjoy yourselves.'

Anna leaves the tent. She thinks, 'Perhaps Maria will be happy to stay with Pablo and the old Prof. Perhaps Ortiz will go to bed very early!' Anna joins the other eight students, and they begin to walk towards Carmen village.

A few minutes later, Pablo comes to Maria's tent. He sits on Anna's bed and talks to Maria. Then they leave the tent, and sit together under a tree at the top of the beach.

Chapter 2

At half-past seven, *they* arrived, out of the sea. Three tall figures; two men and one woman. They wore silver clothes and golden boots. Their faces were dark brown and they had long red hair. Their eyes were very pale and cold.

'They look like bad actors,' said Pablo. 'From some terrible soap opera.'

'No,' replied Maria. 'These are aliens.'

Professor Ortiz was sitting outside his tent. The three strange creatures came up to him.

'What do you want?' said Ortiz.

For a moment, there was silence. Then the woman spoke. 'My name is Kal. This is Thor; and this is Zov.' She pointed to the two men. 'We are from Utopia. Utopia is a planet in the Andromeda galaxy.'

'Oh yes!' said Professor Ortiz. 'Very good!' And he laughed.

'This is not a joke, Professor Ortiz,' said Kal.

'How do you know my name?' said the professor. He was not laughing now.

'We know many things, professor. You come here every year. It is a good idea for your students. This year, there are ten students, plus yourself and your assistant, Pablo Ramon.'

Maria heard everything. She looked at Pablo. Pablo was staring at the scene on the beach. Maria wanted to run, but she didn't move.

Kal spoke again. 'Pablo is there, at the top of the beach, under the tree, with Maria.' The strange woman pointed at Maria. Maria was very frightened.

'What do you want?' asked Professor Ortiz.

'We are alike, you and I,' said Kal. 'We are both collectors.'

'I'm not a collector,' said Professor Ortiz. 'I'm a scientist. I'm here with my students to learn about plant and animal life.'

'Yes, professor. And *we* have studied your little group this afternoon. Now we will choose.'

Maria and Pablo didn't know what happened next. Thor and Zov moved towards them. It was too late to run. Then there was nothing but darkness, and the smell of flowers.

Maria started to wake up. 'What a strange dream!' she thought. She was lying on a bed. She put out her arm, to feel the cold canvas of the tent. 'Anna?' she said. But there was no reply.

Her hand touched the wall. But it wasn't canvas. It was metal. She was not in the tent. Where was she? She put her other hand on the floor. It wasn't sand, or grass. The floor was solid, and covered in straw. Maria opened her eyes. She saw metal bars. She closed her eyes again; the light was very bright. She started to scream: 'Help! Help!' She was very frightened indeed.

No-one came to help Maria. She had no idea where she was.

Finally, Maria opened her eyes again. She looked around. She was in a big room. The room was full of cages. She was in a cage too. The other cages were full of strange animals: silver birds, dogs with feathers, things that looked like cats but had six legs.

Maria turned around. There, on the floor, Pablo was sleeping. Maria screamed very loudly, and started to cry.

The door opened, and Thor and Zov came in. Maria sat in the corner, still crying.

'Ah, the woman is awake,' said Thor.

'But the man is still asleep,' said Zov. 'I hope they will have babies in this cage. Humans are difficult, you know. Do you remember the last couple?'

'Well, they have to eat properly,' said Thor. 'Something more than fish. I think they like something called corn-flakes.'

'Yes, and Coca-Cola to drink. We must go to Atlanta before returning to Utopia.'

Thor moved towards Maria. On a plate, there was a large fish. A red snapper, perhaps. He gave it to her. She dropped the plate and started to scream again. The two aliens left the cage and locked the door. Pablo was still asleep.

The third day of the trip to Carmen Beach was not a success. Professor Ortiz was not well. He had a terrible headache. Some of the students were ill. They had headaches too. The restaurant in Carmen village was cheap, and the wine was very strong. Anna's headache was very bad indeed.

She woke at eleven o'clock. The other bed in the tent was empty. Maria was not there. Anna got up at midday. Nobody had seen Maria.

Anna went to Professor Ortiz's tent. 'Maria has disappeared,' said Anna. 'She didn't come with us last night.'

'Oh – my head!' said Ortiz. 'Maria, you say. Do you mean Maria Gutierrez?'

'Yes.'

'Well, she was very friendly last night with my assistant, Pablo Ramon. He has disappeared too. They will be together. They are young! Leave me alone now.'

That afternoon, the students made up lots of stories about Maria and Pablo. 'They'll be back soon, with big smiles!'

But Maria and Pablo did not come back. In the evening, a student called Fernando returned to Carmen village. He went to the police station. He said that two people had disappeared.

On the fourth and last day of the trip, Carmen Beach was full of policemen. Police-cars searched the land, and helicopters flew over the sea.

Nothing was ever found. Professor Ortiz and the nine remaining students went back to Mexico City. The police decided that Pablo Ramon, twenty-five, and Maria Gutierrez, twenty, were swimming at midnight. Then a shark arrived.

Professor Raul Ortiz was an unhappy man. He liked his assistant, Pablo. Now he didn't have an assistant. And his students learned more slowly. Trips to Carmen Beach were forbidden. 'Real life' was over.

Exercises and Activities

The New Man

1 What is the date when the story begins? What year is it when the story begins – is it possible to say? What happened in 1986? How old was Paul Bryan then? What was Paul's job? Why was he rich? How did things go wrong? How did Diana change?

2 Diana has some ideas about the problems with the factory. Explain her ideas in your own words. Begin like this:

   Diana wants to …

   Why do you think Paul agrees with Diana's plan?

3 You are a policeman at the fire on 15 July 1988. Write a report saying what happened. The following questions will help you to write the report:

   – What time did the fire begin?
   – Where was the body?
   – Who was the dead man?
   – How do you know this?
   – Which room was locked?
   – Which window was broken?

4 Diana is a beautiful but wicked woman. Explain why she is wicked. What did she do? How did she try to do it? Why didn't she completely succeed?

5 Imagine that you are a policewoman. You have come to tell Diana about Paul Bryan's death. Act out the scene between Diana and the policewoman. Then afterwards, write down what Diana is really thinking.

6 Who is Mark Bowler? What does Mark think about:

   – Diana's advertisement in the *Daily Record?*
   – his own face?
   – the body in the toilet?

   Mark is the 'New Man'. He marries Diana. Does he love Diana?

Why does he marry her? Why does Mark feel lucky? Why doesn't he go to the police?

7 Who is Jimmy? What is his job? Why does Mark phone Jimmy and say, 'Both the cars will be in the garage?' What does Mark want Jimmy to do? What actually happens? Why does Diana say 'Well done!' to Jimmy?

8 Imagine that Jimmy is now married to Diana. Write the story of *The New Man* from Jimmy's point of view. Write at least two paragraphs.

Cell 13

1 As you read the story make a list of all the people named. Write down the date(s) in March when they are mentioned. Also, write down who these people are and what you know about them.

Example:
Jackson – 1 March and 3 March. Jackson was in cell 13 with Jason Hill.

The name of the prisoner in cell 13 is Jason Hill.

2 On 3 March Jason writes, 'There are noises in the night.' On 9 March he writes, 'I am alone in cell 13 with a ghost.' Describe what happens between 3 March and 9 March. Begin like this:

On 4 March Jason hears noises ...

3 Jason makes a model ship. What does he make it from? Who gives him these things? When does he begin the model? Why does he make it? What happens to the ship? Why do you think this happens?

4 Complete the following sentences, using one word:

Example:
This is the diary .... a young prisoner.

This is the diary of a young prisoner.

a Jason killed himself .... prison.

b Jason couldn't sleep .... night.

c Jason received a letter .... his girlfriend.

d He made the model ship .... the evenings.

e The prison officer opened the door .... his cell.

f Jason talked .... the priest about his problem.

g He was terrified .... the ghost.

5 Describe the ghost. What happens between 10 March and 13 March? Why do you think Jason hangs himself?

6 Do you believe in ghosts? Discuss this question in groups of three or four. Give reasons for your opinions. Then write at least one paragraph about the subject. The following phrases will help you:

Example:
I believe in ghosts because ...
I (don't) believe in life after death ...
I (don't) think that ghosts exist ...
People can easily imagine things at night ...

Carmen Beach

Chapter 1

1 Why are the students spending four days at Carmen Beach? How does Maria feel about the trip? Why does she feel like this? Who is Pablo?

Describe in your own words what Pablo sees over the Gulf. What does the professor see? What does Pablo think the object is? Why can't Maria speak? What happens to the weather?

2   What do you think is going to happen next? Discuss this in
     groups of two or three. Give reasons for your opinions.

     Example:
     I think (that) Pablo is going to ...
     I think (that) the spaceship will ...
     I think Maria is going to ...
     I think this will happen because ...

Chapter 2

3   'They arrived, out of the sea.' Who are 'they'? Where are they
     from? What are they wearing? What colour is their hair? What
     do they want? Why do they say to Professor Ortiz, 'We are both
     collectors'? When Maria wakes up, where is she? Who is with
     her? What is she given to eat? What do the police decide?

4   Complete the following sentences with a verb in the past simple
     tense.

     Example:
     Pablo .... something in the sky.
     Pablo saw something in the sky.

     a Maria .... bad about the trip.
     b Pablo and Maria .... under a tree on the beach.
     c The aliens .... Maria and Pablo in a cage.
     d Professor Ortiz never .... to Carmen Beach again.
     e The professor .... the spaceship was a weather
        balloon.
     f The aliens .... Maria a red snapper to eat.
     g The aliens .... from a planet in the Andromeda
        galaxy.

5   Write a diary for Professor Ortiz for the four days of his trip to
     Carmen Beach. Write at least one paragraph for each day.

6   Which is your favourite story in this book: *The New Man, Cell 13*
     or *Carmen Beach?* Which is the story you like least? Discuss these
     two questions in groups of four. Give reasons for your opinions.

Example:
My favourite story is …
I like it best because …
It's my favourite because …
The story I like least is …
This is because …

Glossary

The New Man

avoid   to keep away from
burn   to destroy by fire
champagne   A French wine; people drink it when they want to
celebrate
car crash   a car accident; when a car goes violently into something
escape   to get away from a difficult situation
factory   a building where things are made by machine, for sale
false   not real
firm   strong
fool   a stupid person
grave(stone)   the place where a dead person is put in the earth; a
stone usually marks the grave
insurance   money paid to a company; if something goes wrong in
your life, the company will then pay you money
mechanic   a person who works with machines, especially cars
mirror   a piece of glass that reflects things
policy   a written agreement with a company
tear(s)   water that comes from the eyes, because of pain or sadness
tramp   a person without a home or job
widow   a woman whose husband is dead

Cell 13

diary   a notebook in which you write about your life, from day to
day
dream   a story that you imagine while you are asleep
chapel   a small church or room, used for Christian religious services
ghost   the spirit of someone who has died
governor   the head, boss of a prison
hang(ed)   to die by falling, with a rope around the neck
lawyer   a person who advises people about the law
library   a room with books that people can borrow
match(es)   a small stick of wood, used to make fire
noise(s)   a sound

prison   a large building where criminals must live
can't stand   to find something impossible to accept; to hate
terrified   very frightened

Carmen Beach

Chapter 1

biology   the scientific study of living things
clam(s)   a small, soft sea animal, with a shell
disappear   to leave or become lost, without explanation
funny   strange, surprising
tent   a shelter made of cloth or plastic; when you camp you sleep in
   a tent
trip   a journey for a particular purpose
space   what is outside the Earth's air; where the stars and
   planets are
weather balloon   an object in the sky that measures changes in the
      climate

Chapter 2

alien(s)   a person who do not live on the Earth; a creature from
      another planet
bar   a long, thin piece of metal
cage   a box or room with bars, to contain animals (as in zoos)
canvas   strong cloth; the material used to make tents
corn-flakes   a type of cereal, usually eaten at breakfast
forbidden   not allowed, not permitted
shark   a very big, dangerous fish, which sometimes attacks people
a red snapper   a type of fish
soap opera   a daily or weekly continuing television story
straw   dry, yellow grass